T5-CVF-565

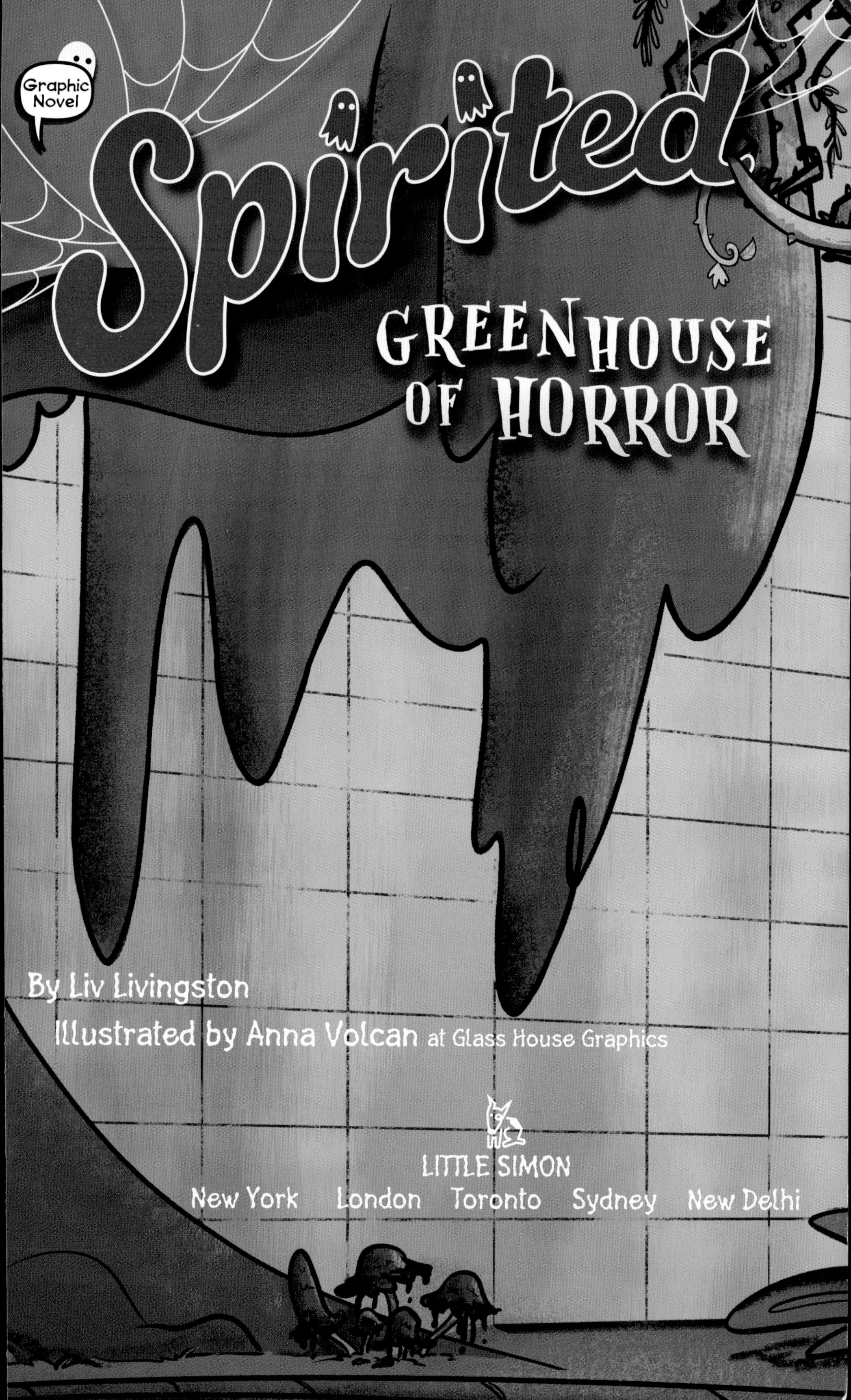

Spirited
GREENHOUSE OF HORROR

By Liv Livingston
Illustrated by Anna Volcan at Glass House Graphics

LITTLE SIMON
New York London Toronto Sydney New Delhi

This book is a work of fiction. Any references to historical events, real people, or real places are used fictitiously. Other names, characters, places, and events are products of the author's imagination, and any resemblance to actual events or places or persons, living or dead, is entirely coincidental.

LITTLE SIMON
An imprint of Simon & Schuster Children's Publishing Division
1230 Avenue of the Americas, New York, New York 10020
First Little Simon edition July 2024

Simon & Schuster: Celebrating 100 Years of Publishing in 2024
For information about special discounts for bulk purchases, please contact Simon & Schuster Special Sales at 1-866-506-1949 or business@simonandschuster.com.
The Simon & Schuster Speakers Bureau can bring authors to your live event. For more information or to book an event, contact the Simon & Schuster Speakers Bureau at 1-866-248-3049 or visit our website at www.simonspeakers.com.
Cover by Manuel Preitano. Illustrated by Anna Volcan at Glass House Graphics. Layouts by Giulia Balsamo. Colors by Antonino Ulizzi, Vanessa Costanzo, and Nataliya Torretta. Lettering by Giovanni Spadaro/Grafimated Cartoon. Supervision by Salvatore Di Marco/ Grafimated Cartoon.
Designed by Brittany Fetcho
Manufactured in China 0324 SCP
2 4 6 8 10 9 7 5 3 1
Library of Congress Cataloging-in-Publication Data
Names: Livingston, Liv, author. | Glass House Graphics, illustrator.
Title: Greenhouse of horror / by Liv Livingston ; illustrated by Glass House Graphics.
Description: First Little Simon edition. | New York : Little Simon, 2024.
Series: Spirited ; book 3 | Audience: Ages 5–9 |
Summary: Liv meets Mrs. Arber, the ghost caring for the Gloomsdale Botanical Gardens who has come to help Liv's class with their class project, which asks that the students find a plant that best represents them, but Liv has trouble knowing the answer.
Identifiers: LCCN 2023032582 (print) | LCCN 2023032583 (ebook)
ISBN 9781665956970 (paperback) | ISBN 9781665956987 (hardcover)
ISBN 9781665956994 (ebook)
Subjects: CYAC: Graphic novels. | Ghosts—Fiction. | Plants—Fiction. | Schools—Fiction. | LCGFT: Paranormal comics. | Graphic novels.
Classification: LCC PZ7.7.L596 Gr 2024 (print) | LCC PZ7.7.L596 (ebook) |
DDC 741.5/973—dc23/eng/20230922
LC record available at https://lccn.loc.gov/2023032582
LC ebook record available at https://lccn.loc.gov/2023032583

Contents

CHAPTER 1

Have you ever seen a ghost?

Or ever spoken
to one?
Well, if
you have...
...you might
understand that
living in a town of
ghosts can get really
weird, really fast.

Trust me...
...I know what I'm talking about.
Hi. I'm Olivia Livingston, but you can call me Liv.
And here are just SOME examples of my strange new life...

...in my strange new ghost town, Gloomsdale!

Sometimes I couldn't reach my homeroom...
Ugh. Not this again!
...because the door LITERALLY floats in the air!
All the other kids got in just fine, of course.
Come on, Living Liv! Just float up!

Just float?
Yeah, no such luck.
I had to wait for the janitor to bring me a ladder. Every. Single. Time.

Thanks!
Grunt.
He never really says much, but I know he's cool.
Whew.
She's so weird.
Like, in a funny way, Liv.
Sure, Astrid. Whatever you say.
She didn't mean I was "funny." She meant I wasn't ghostly.

Strangeness Example Number Two:
That time with my little sister, Amelia, at the park.
We slid down the slide normally... or so I thought!

Liv...
do you not
know how
to slide?
I guess
we'll have to
show her!

Yeah. The
ghosts slid UP
the slide!

See? It's
like THAT.
Uh...

LIKE THIS! SEE, LIV?
Do you want a turn?

Here we goooooooo!!!
ACK!

See? This is how you have fun!
Riiight. I'll remember for...next time. You know, for when I learn how to float.

And, of course, Strangeness Example Number Three:
Don't even get me STARTED on the number of times ghost kids "accidentally" go through me in the hall.
Ugh!

It's SO MANY TIMES.

NOPE! DON'T EVEN THINK ABOUT IT!

But it's funny...
No float-throughs for ANYBODY!
Awww...
It's like getting a brain freeze! Blech!
SCIENCE IS SPOOOOKY
So you see, sometimes a girl just wants to be left alone in her normalness.

But honestly? It seemed like being normal in a town full of ghosts was never going to happen.
Life Cycle
PHY
We will begin a very exciting chapter today, students. Along with our special guest teacher, I hope you're ALL excited for a day of...
PHYTOLOGY
...PHYTOLOGY!!!!

Fi-do-what???

PHYTOLOG
Ah, let me try that again.

I hope you're excited for...

GREENHOUSE

THE GREENHOUSE!!!

It's that time of year!!!
I had no idea what he meant by that, but everybody's excitement was catching.
My older sister's best friend's cousin tried smelling a flower from the greenhouse once, and it got stuck up her nose, and, well... the rest is *ghostory!*
I can't wait to see how pointy the mega-sharp rose thorns will get!!!
Up her nose? Ghostory? Mega-sharp?

Let us go! Plants, here we come!

Eek! I heard this year's poison ivy is EXTRA poisonous!!!

Wait a second...

Exactly how dangerous is plant life in Gloomsdale???

CHAPTER 2
I didn't know much about plants, besides the fact that they need water and sunlight.

I mean, how much could there be to learn?
PLANTED BY THE GARDENING CLUB
They're pretty. They don't always smell as nice as people say they do.
Oh, and my parents can't keep plants alive.

Not even
a cactus.
Trust
me, a cactus
needs A LOT
of water!
I think
I read the
instructions
wrong...
So when it came to the
school's greenhouse...
I had no idea what
was coming.

Whoa...
Come on in, everybody! Float on by—quickly, quickly!

Oops!
BUMP
Oops!

I'm so sorry! I didn't see you there!
It's okay!

Really, I'm so sorry, Liv!

It's fine! Really! What's...

...I was pretty sure this
one wasn't normal at all.
It was big...
...and spooky...
...and unlike anything
I'd ever seen.

As you may know, this is a school-wide assignment. All students will be participating in this most green project!
GLOVES
BOO!
Gotcha!
Vera! Hey!

I'm so glad you're here.
Howl's here too.

The whole school does it each year! Oh, you'll just love Mrs. Arber! She helps run the Gloomsdale Botanical Gardens.
Yeah, she's been around for AGES.

Gloomsdale Botanical Gardens
HOWLWARD MOON, JUNIOR!!!!
Gloomsdale Botanical Gardens
Sorry, Mrs. Arber...
POOF
Okay, maybe it wasn't the best choice I've ever made.

To be fair, you've made a *lot* of bad choices.
Hey now!
Um...you guys...

Is that a... ghost???

Duh!

We're ALL ghosts, Liv! Well, MOST of us.

UGH!!!
GROSS!!!

And THAT is why we must protect our clothing while working with certain plants!
First lesson learned.
Now, who wants to get their hands dirty? Or should I say *dirtier*?
Yep. Definitely not your average plants.

CHAPTER 3
Welcome to the greenhouse, children of nature!
I am Mrs. Arber, and it is a pleasure to be here!
Today and always, we shall be students of the natural *and* unnatural worlds.
Ugh, we know, we know. We're students for, like, *ever*...

Each year, the students of Gloomsdale come together for a very special project.
Can anyone tell me what it is?
Flower bed.
What was that? Float up a bit so I can hear you better, my dear.

The special project is a student-designed flower bed.
Correct! Thank you, Eri! I wouldn't expect anything less from our Gardening Club president.
So that was her name... Eri!
Now, come along, students!

Watch out for the poison ivy!
Oh my, look how much the baneberry has grown!

Oooh, those are pretty.
Thank you!
What do you mean...?
Vera & HOWL
Wait. You both did this?
Howl and I worked on it last year!
Vera & HOWL

And now here's your assignment! Tomorrow, each student will bring in a plant that best represents them. You shall present the plant to the class...
...and then I will help you plant it in this year's plot!
Can we use the same plant as last year?
Time has passed and your roots are deeper. Try to find what else is blooming within you!
I have something to say!
Astrid Sneer. Whenever she spoke, I immediately got goose bumps. And NOT just because of her ghostliness. She was cold and snarky through and through.

Yes, Miss Sneer?
Ahem.
LISTEN UP! HERE'S A CHEER! TRUST ME, IT'S ONE YOU'LL WANNA HEAR!
SHE'S GROWN! ASTRID SNEER! YOU BET I'LL HAVE A NEW PLANT THIS YEAR!

WOOO-HOOO!!!
GO, GHOUL, GO!
She's *grown*? She's the exact same height she's *always* been!
Er...thank you, Miss Sneer.

Does anyone else have a question?
I can't wait to bring mine in!
All good, Mr. S!
Nah, I got this!
Sooo...Howl and I are going to the plant shop after school.

Wanna come with us?
It's a short walk into town. My mom's coming too!
Okay!
Wait. I'll have to let my parents know.
No problem!
We'll send them a message by bat!
Okay, sometimes this ghost stuff was handy.

Your parents will get the message in no time.
Yay!
Double yay!
Maybe this plant stuff wouldn't be so bad!
I mean, how hard could it be?

Ooh!

Watch your see-through backs, ghosts! I've got this in the bag...

...I think.
HISS

Wait up, you two!!!

CHAPTER 4

Home is where the heart blooms.

At least, that's what Mrs. Arber liked to teach me.

But right then, among all the other Gloomsdale students, I wasn't sure when I was going to bloom.

Or where. Or even IF!

Just like Vera said, my parents received my message in no time...and responded just as quickly.
YOU CAN GO! HAVE FUN! WE DIDN'T KNOW BATS COULD DELIVER MAIL! MOM &
There's Mrs. Moon!
Mooooooooom.
I thought we agreed: no more wolfing around in front of my friends!!!
POOF
Don't be silly. There's nothing better than being wolfy!
Yeah, Howl's mom was pretty awesome.

Ugh.

You girls ready?

Hi, Mrs. Moon!!!

GLOOM'S SCHOOL

Yeah! Let's go buy some plants!

I hadn't really taken the time to walk through Gloomsdale before that day.

But the more I saw...
Lemonades
...the more I realized this town was just like any other.
WELCOME to DOWNTOWN GLOOMSDALE! A Great Haunt
Well, *almost* like any other.

There were clothing stores...
BOUTIQUE
SALE on the LATEST STYLES
...restaurants...
Restaurant
GOULash
OPEN

...that one hat store
Mom is obsessed with...

Tip-Top
MILLINER SHOP

Delightful!
Waflllavrrrrrizzzzt???
MMMMM!!!
He means, what flavor is it?

Spiders and cobwebs!

Oh, I'm just joking! It is simply made with red plums!
I knew it tasted familiar!
Whew.
Haha. Ghosts sure can joke, I guess.

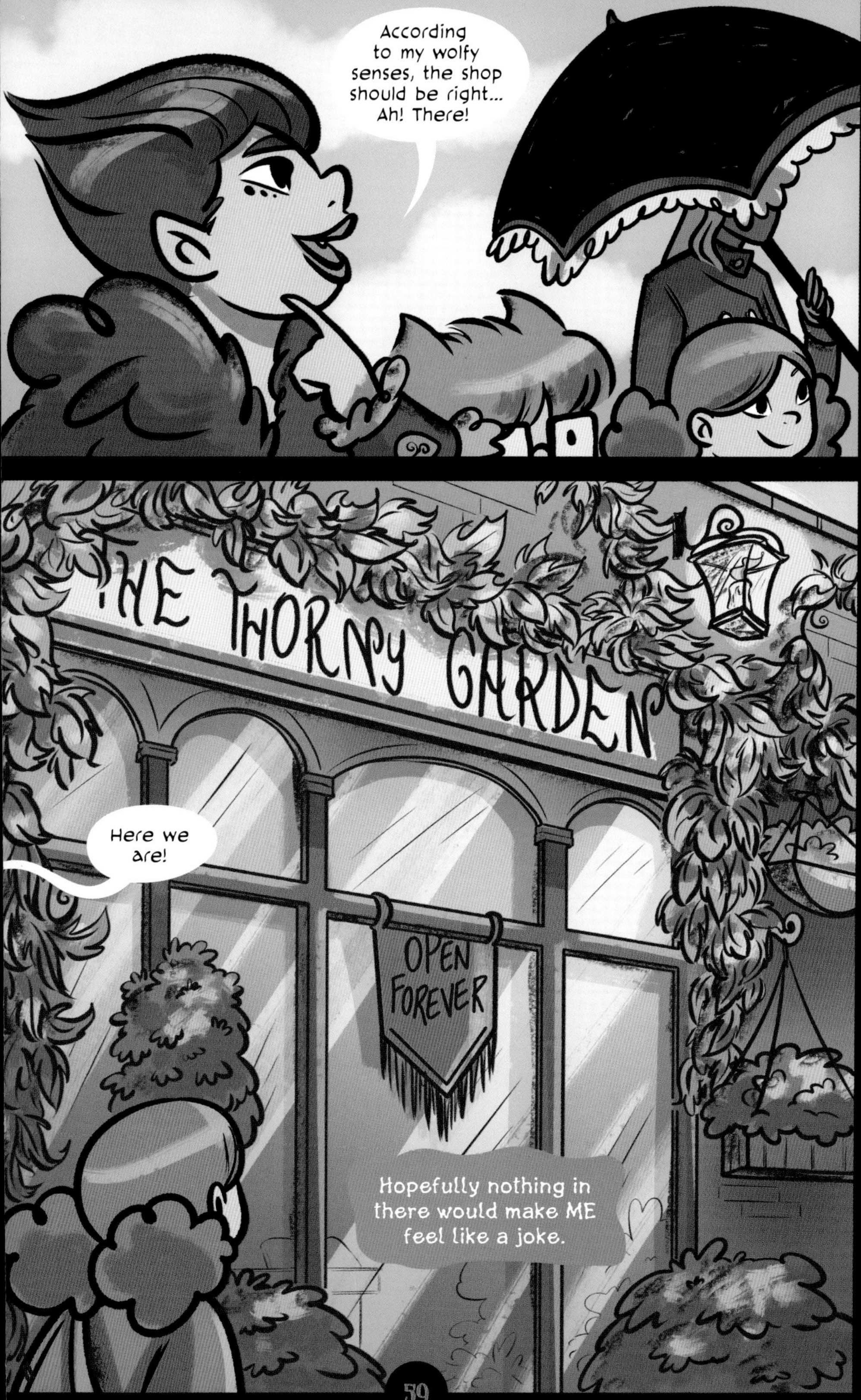
According to my wolfy senses, the shop should be right... Ah! There!
THE THORNY GARDEN
Here we are!
OPEN FOREVER
Hopefully nothing in there would make ME feel like a joke.

CHAPTER 5
DING
Turns out, the joke was on me...Just like the greenhouse, there was nothing normal in this whole place.

Okay, you kids look around. I'm going to run back to the bakery to pick up some peanut butter treats for your brothers, Howl.
I like peanut butter treats *too.*
Of course you do, my sweet pup. Not to worry, I'll get treats for the whole family!

Have fun! Don't get eaten by anything in here!

Um.
She was joking... right?

Wow. This looks...

So red! It's beautiful!
Keep it cool, vamp.

POOF
Greetings!! Welcome to the Thorny Garden, the most beautiful shop in town!
Hi, Iris!
Whoa!
Please, feel free to peruse!
What is that AMAZING scent? I can't quite place it...

Ahhh, it's the sweet peas just over here!

I've never seen something so...so... DIVINE!

I don't believe we've met before, young ghostling.

Oh right.

This is Olivia Livingston, the new kid in town!
Liv, this is Iris. She knows everything there is to know about plants.
Liv is our first-ever 100-percent-human Living Girl!!
GASP!!!
This is...this is...ABSOLUTELY MAGICAL!!!
It is?

Liv is simply the greatest!
Yeah. Oh, um...a little help here?
That's enough from you!
Thanks!
Anyway, we're here for our school project. You know, the same as last year?

Why, of course! This is my favorite time of the year! Everyone always has such incredible ideas.
One year I brought in a plant that had a dozen bats hanging off it!
I'd like to bring something different in, but— oooh, I just love this color!
Did Vera and Howl already know what they wanted?
Would they have to wait around for me to decide what plant best suited me?

Some of them were too big. Others a little too gloomy. And there were so many options.
TOO many.
Any chance... you could walk us through some options? I'm not quite sure what I want yet.
A plant fashion show?

Oh yes, yes, yes!

We'll start with this beauty right here!
It's your line, kids.
What's that plant?

Here we have a classic BLACK ROSE!
It stands for love, friendship, and new beginnings! Just watch out for the thorns!
Ouch! Heh. Told ya.
So, what do you think?
Too pointy.

No problem. How about...

...this one?

What's that plant?

Here we have...a SNAKE PLANT!!! Tall, strong, and it fights off bad luck!

HSSSSSSSSSSS!!!
That's a little too snaky for me.

Liv here is an artist. How about something totally showstopping?

Hmmm...a real showstopper...

Gasp!
I've got it!

...What's that plant?

Beware, for this plant is unlike any other.
It is...
Could this be my plant? Would this outshine all the others? Would everyone FINALLY take me seriously?
WHOOOSH

THE TITAN ARUM!!!
WHAAAT?

CHAPTER 6
Oh...
My...
Ghoulness.

It is a bit much, isn't it?

Oh! I know just the one! It's a sweet little bug-eating plant!

Got it!
It even sings a haunting little tune!
Bug-eating plant? Haunting tune?

CHOMP
Rotten-fly alert!

DING
SNIFF SNIFF
Iris, did you let the bug chewer eat another gross fly again—? OH!

Hi...
Hey, little sister! Finally back from Gardening Club? Maybe you can help your school friends find a plant!
Okay...
Liv isn't quite finding what she needs. Maybe...your secret collection can help?
Oh, I don't know...
Don't be shy! Go on!

It's...um...
this way.
I would
join you,
but...
These cuddle
vines really like
a warm hug!
If you tickle
them, they let
go. Like this!
Okay, you go
on. We'll catch up
in a minute, Liv!

Are you sure this is okay?
Yeah, it's no big deal. Oh, but watch out for the bags of dirt.
My collection's just back here.

So...both you and your sister are really into plants, huh?
Yeah!
Just a sec. This poison hemlock is getting a little dry.
Sure, yeah... can't let that... poison...get droopy.
Or maybe you *should.* But I would never tell a plant lover that.

Iris owns the store, and I help out. Sometimes I bring the Gardening Club here to do fundraising for the school garden.
Very cool.
Okay, it's back this way...
The plants seem to like you a lot. I bet that makes you a pretty great Gardening Club president.

I'm glad at least one person thinks so.
What do you mean?
The other club members and I don't really like the same things.
But you all like plants, right?
Well, sure. It's just...they're super into Gloomsdale's plants. But I...well, I like these instead.
CREEEEEK

ERI'S GROVE
This...is beautiful!

You really think so?
Definitely! I actually recognize these plants!
They're perfect!
Daisies, sunflowers, cosmos...

But not everyone appreciates them, no matter how many times I try to plant them at school.
I'll never really fit in, anyway. I mean, THEY won't fit in— the flowers, ha! Not...not me.
Hmm.
What?
I don't think that's quite true.
I mean... just look at *me.* I didn't think I'd ever make friends at Gloomsdale. But luckily, I did. And I'm still meeting new ones, like you.

I guess you're right. Everything eventually finds its place.
It's just hard not to feel like a weed growing through the sidewalk sometimes.
I hadn't realized until then that even though the other kids at school were ghosts...
...sometimes *they* could feel like the odd ghoul out too.

Eri, I think
I know what
we're doing for
our project.
OUR
project?

CHAPTER 7

When I arrived at school the next day, I couldn't wait for science class.

Even though I knew my project was unexpected, there was no denying it was fully ME.

STEWART THE STEWARD:
Principal's assistant.
Expert trumpeter.

Questioner
of plants.
Whoa, whoa,
WHOA! What is
that thing?

What thing?
Oh, you mean Astrid?
Rude!
I meant, what is *that?*
It's the plant that best represents me!

Do you like it?
Well...
It's very... different.
STEWART! JUST WHAT IS GOING ON HERE?

WHY HAVEN'T YOU BROUGHT ME MY HOT COCOA—WHOA!

PRINCIPAL REGINALD: Principal. King of some unknown realm.

Also a questioner of plants.

So what if that wasn't the best reaction? It's not like they were in my class. So it didn't matter!
Right?
...Right?

That sure is tiny, Liv. Does it suddenly become bigger at night?
No.

I don't see any thorns. Is it at least poisonous?
NO.
It's so...GREEN. You were supposed to do it like THIS, Liv!
My plant is just fine the way it is!
Okay, maybe Stewart and Principal Reginald had been trying to warn me. Maybe I should've listened.

Make way!
Hi, Liv! Oooh, is that your project???

You never did show us what it was once we left the shop yesterday.
I'm going to wait until class. You know, as a surprise!
Cool! I can't wait to find out!
I totally didn't need Vera telling me my plant was weird too.
All right class, let's talk about verbs, shall we? But not just any verbs... ones that float off sentences!
I just needed to get through my classes.

Time to
show you off,
plant!

The moment I showed up to science class, I felt like those cuddle vines from Iris's shop were wrapping around me.
Oh well. Just another day in the life of Living Liv.

CHAPTER 8
Maybe it was time to face the thorny facts.
Maybe I wasn't a REAL Gloomsdale student.

Are you ready to present your unbeLEAFable projects?
YES!
Where was Eri?
Had she changed her mind about doing our project together? I sure hoped not, or this would be mega-awkward.

There was no going back now!

Okay, then—who's first?

Ready?

Okay!

This is the black mondo grass, which has traveled with my family line throughout the ages as we cheered on epic battles and as boats pushed off into the water for the first time.

That's right! This fella was the inspiration for the first-ever pom-pom!
Basically, without the Sneers, there wouldn't even be cheers!

Goooooooo, SNEERS!
POOF
POOF

WOOO-HOOOOOO!!!

Where was Eri???

Next up was Vera. As always, she was totally cool.
This is the bat-faced flower! As you can see, it is red and purple, my FAVORITE colors!

Then it was Howl's turn. He was, as always, a total pup.
This is my special flower bed with grass. Whenever I'm feeling sick or nervous, I just chew up some grass and then my tummy feels better! Just like any other werepup!
I mean, wereWOLF.

And were you feeling nervous today?
Maybe.
Howl wasn't the only nervous one.
Eri still wasn't here. What was I going to do with only half of our project?

Other kids kept raising their hands, while I kept scooting farther and farther toward the back of the group.
There was the brainlike cactus...
...a bunch of brown flowers that looked like my great-aunt's fancy hair...

...something called
snappy dragons...
I really hoped they
didn't breathe fire.
...and everything else that
looked nothing like mine.

Wonderful job, class! That brings us to the last two students...
Miss Livingston. Would you like to go next?
Uh...

I'm here! I'm here!
Sorry! The cuddle vines needed extra cuddling this morning, but I made it!!!

We worked on something together! If that's okay?
We cannot *wait* to see, dears. Go on.

CHAPTER 9

We are proud to present to you...
...a very special arrangement of...
WEEDS!

Oooohhh!
Weeds? Why would you choose to bring THOSE?
Isn't Eri the Gardening Club president? I thought she'd bring something super spooky!
Not quite so much audience participation, please!

And what do these plants mean to you, ladies?
Um... well...they mean...
They mean that you don't have to be like others to belong. Right, Eri?
Right!
You see, weeds grow in places where people think they won't do well.

But they're survivors!
And eventually... they thrive!
But that's not all! If you give them a little time...

...they become something magical.

Oooh!!!
Aaah!!!

Okay, even I have to admit that was cute.

Ick. Did I just say that?
C-U-T-E!

Soon, class, you'll see how right these girls are, for love and support can make anything grow.
Very, very well done, ladies!
CLAP CLAP CLAP CLAP

Best president EVER!

Go, Eri!

That's the end of the presentations, and you know what that means, class...
TIME TO GET MESSY!!!!!

HOWL!!!

Liv
Eri
Howl
Vera
Plants have taught me a few things. They've taught me that sometimes we're so worried about what we're doing *differently* that we don't realize everything we're doing *just right.*

CHAPTER 10
A few weeks later...
I couldn't help myself.
I just *had* to arrive at school early to check on the plants.

Oh! You're here early!
PLANTS! GOTTA GO! SEE!
Okaaaay...?

Little weeds...
Here...
I...
Come!!!

Hey,
you.

Some days, I can't help but feel as if I don't belong.
But I guess everyone feels like that sometimes.
Ghost or human. Werewolf or vampire.

Getting used to a new home and new friends isn't easy.
But these days...

Here we go...

Liv?
I'm here!
Yeah, these days I know...

...we'll be
just fine.

Can't get enough of

Spirited?

Check out the next adventure...